W9-CBP-672

JUST A SPECIAL THANKSGIVING

BY MERCER MAYER

HARPER FESTIVAL
An Imprint of HarperCollinsPublishers

www.harpercollinschildrens.com
ISBN 978-0-06-147811-6
15 16 17 18 19   CWM   10 9 8 7 6 5 4 3
❖

 A Big Tuna Trading Company, LLC/J. R. Sansevere Book
www.harpercollinschildrens.com   www.littlecritter.com
First Edition

It was the last day of school before the Thanksgiving holiday.

My class was making projects to take home.

Tiger said my turkey looked like a pumpkin.

I said Tiger's pilgrim looked like a fence post with scribbles.

Everyone laughed.

Miss Kitty said, "Time to clean up. Don't forget the school play tonight."

The bell rang and it was time to go home.

That evening I got ready for the play.
Mom helped me put on my costume.
I was a turkey.

We drove to school and I went backstage to wait.

I looked out at the audience.
There were so many critters,
I got butterflies in my tummy.

The curtain went up and the play began.

When it was my turn to say something, I forgot my lines.
I was just so nervous.

So I surprised everyone and sang a song instead.

I think they liked it because they all clapped.

The play was finally over and I was happy to go home.

I was so tired I fell asleep without a story for the first time ever.

The next morning I got up early.
It was the big Thanksgiving Day Parade.

The Critter Scout troop and I were
marching in our costumes from the play.

After a while I was tired.
I climbed up on a float. I could see
everything.
"Hi, Mom! Hi, Dad!" I called.
They didn't look too happy.

Mr. Policeman helped me down.
He took me to the lost and found, and I
found my mom, my dad, and Little Sister.

We went home after all that.
Mom was very mad. Dad was too, and my
little sister couldn't stop laughing.

After dinner we went shopping for the turkey and stuff.

"See how strong I am," I said. "Oops!" I dropped the turkey.

"Don't worry, Mom. I can brush it off."

"We need cranberries, Dad," I called.
I grabbed them up and Little Sister held the bag.

I missed the bag.
I called, "How 'bout some help, huh, Dad?"

The next day, we were up early.
Everybody helped prepare the feast.

Finally the turkey was ready.
Dad said, "We are having a surprise dinner."
We cleaned up and took the turkey to the car.

We drove to the community center.
Everyone from town was there.
Mom told us that the town decided to have a big
community Thanksgiving dinner.

They invited all the critters who couldn't have a nice dinner.
This way everyone could enjoy it together.

Little Sister and I helped serve the food.
It was fun. The food was yummy. "Wow," I said.
"This was really a special Thanksgiving!"